# Ruby Flew Too!

Happy 1st
Birthday
Gorgeous Girl
xxx

For Isabelle
JE

In loving memory of my
wonderful mum, Tanya xxx
RH

First published 2004 as *Once Upon a Time Upon a Nest* by Macmillan Children's Books
This edition published 2005 by Macmillan Children's Books
a division of Macmillan Publishers Limited
20 New Wharf Road, London N1 9RR
Basingstoke and Oxford
Associated companies throughout the world
www.panmacmillan.com

ISBN-13: 978-1-4050-5162-0
ISBN-10: 1-4050-5162-0

Text copyright © Jonathan Emmett 2004
Illustrations copyright © Rebecca Harry 2004
Moral rights asserted.
You can find out more about Jonathan Emmett's books
at www.scribblestreet.co.uk

7 9 8 6

A CIP catalogue record for this book is available from the British Library.

Printed in China

# Ruby Flew Too!

Written by
## Jonathan Emmett

Illustrated by
## Rebecca Harry

MACMILLAN CHILDREN'S BOOKS

Once upon a time,
upon a nest,
beside a lake,
there lived two ducks.

A mother duck

and a father duck.

There were five eggs in
the nest. Mother Duck sat
upon the nest,

all day...

and all night...

Through howling
wind . . .

and driving rain,
looking after the
eggs. ALL five
of them.

Then, one bright morning,
the eggs began to hatch.

One

two

three

four

little beaks poked out
into the sunlight.

**One**

**two**

**three**

**four** little ducklings shook
their feathers in
the breeze.

"We'll call them
Rufus, Rory, Rosie and
Rebecca," said Father Duck.
And Mother Duck agreed.

But the fifth egg did **nothing**.

"Will it **ever** hatch?"
said Father Duck.

"It will," said
Mother Duck,
"in its own time."

And –
sure enough –

it did.

"She's very small,"
said Father Duck.
"What shall we call her?"

"We'll call her Ruby,"
said Mother Duck,
"because she's small
and precious."

Rufus, Rory, Rosie and Rebecca
ate whatever they were given.

They ate anything
and **everything**.

But Ruby ate
**nothing**.

"Will she
**ever** eat?"
said Father Duck.

"She will," said
Mother Duck,
"in her own time."

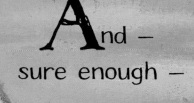

And –
sure enough –

she did.

Rufus, Rory, Rosie and Rebecca
swam off whenever they
were able.

They swam
anywhere

and
everywhere.

But Ruby swam
nowhere.

"Will she ever swim?" said Father Duck.
"She will," said Mother Duck,
"in her own time."

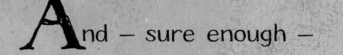

**A**nd – sure enough –

she did.

Rufus, Rory, Rosie
and Rebecca
grew
**bigger.**

And Ruby grew
**bigger** too.
Her feathers grew
out and her wings grew
broad and beautiful.

And when

and Rebecca
began to
fly...

Rosie

Rory

Rufus

. . . Ruby flew too!

Rufus, Rory, Rosie
and Rebecca flew far
and wide. They flew out,
across the water.
They flew up, among
the trees.

But Ruby flew farther and wider.
She flew out, **beyond** the water.

She flew up, **above** the trees.

She flew anywhere
and **everywhere**.

She stretched out her beautiful wings . . .

and soared high among the clouds.

Mother Duck and Father Duck
watched Ruby flying off
into the distance.

"Will she ever come back?"
said Mother Duck.
"She will," said Father Duck,
"in her own time."

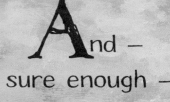

And –
sure enough –

SHE DID.